The Day The Dog First Called

AMY LAURENS

OTHER WORKS

SANCTUARY SERIES

Where Shadows Rise
Through Roads Between
When Worlds Collide

KADITEOS SERIES

How Not To Acquire A Castle

STORM FOXES SERIES

A Fox of Storms and Starlight
A Stag Of Hope And Memory

SHORTER WORKS

Darkness And Good
Dreaming Of Forests
It All Changes Now
Of Sea Foam And Blood
Rush Job
Trust Issues

NON-FICTION

How To Write Dogs
How To Theme
How To Create Cultures
How To Create Life
How To Map
The 32 Worst Mistakes People Make About Dogs

Find other works by the author at www.amylaurens.com

The Day The Dog

First Called

INKLET #51

AMY LAURENS

www.inkprintpress.com

Print ISBN: 978-1-925825-53-4
eBook ISBN: 9781393494140

www.inkprintpress.com

National Library of Australia Cataloguing-in-Publication Data
Laurens, Amy 1985 –
The Day The Dog First Called
48 p.
ISBN: 978-1-925825-53-4
Inkprint Press, Canberra, Australia
1. Fiction—Fantasy—Dark 2. Fiction—Fantasy—Contemporary 3. Fiction—Women 4. Fiction—Short Stories

First Print Edition: February 2021
Cover design © Inkprint Press
Interior art © Amy Laurens

THE DAY THE DOG
FIRST CALLED

The day the dog first called, Natalia had been contemplating suicide. The cobwebby blackness that had once been confined to the upper corners of the house had recently begun to send out feelers and criss-cross the ceiling, and she knew it wouldn't be too much longer before they reached down the walls and engulfed the floor, and then nowhere would be safe and she might as well be dead. Fear, however, held her back, and she was just contemplating her own futility when the doorbell rang.

Ordinarily, when the cobwebs pressed down and she couldn't breathe, Natalia ignored the doorbell—and the phone—but today, morbid as her thoughts were, she thought perhaps she might like to share them with someone. And so she answered the door.

"What do you think," she began, intending to question the visitor about means and methods, and stopped: the visitor was a shaggy, dirty-white dog. "Oh," Natalia finished instead. "I expect you don't think much about anything, do you."

The dog sat, pink tongue lolling to one side, and stared at her. "Well," it said. "I hope sometimes I do."

Natalia stared back. "I suppose you had better come in, then," she said at last. "Can't have you sit there all day."

The dog stood, and she motioned it into the house. It waited politely in the entryway for her to close the door, then followed her into the kitchen.

"Would you like a drink?" Natalia asked, moving stacks of dirty bowls onto piles of used plates. After all, a talking dog was no stranger than the cobwebs, and it never hurt to be polite. "Sorry about the mess."

"Not at all," replied the dog. "Some water would be lovely."

Natalia rummaged in the cupboards for something clean, settling at last on a greasy glass baking dish. Turning away, she gave it a quick polish with a tea towel that had seen better days and hoped the dog wouldn't mind. She filled it with cool water and set it on the floor.

"Thank you," the dog said, and lapped at it.

Natalia leaned back against the kitchen sink, watching the rhythmic motions of his mouth and overtly ignoring the black feeler that waved in her peripheral vision. Her husband had said ignoring her 'strange fantasies' might improve the situation, and while it had never worked yet, she felt she ought to at least make an effort in the presence of a guest.

The dog finished and raised his head, water dripping from his hairy chin. He glanced around and gestured at a second dirty tea towel lying crumpled on the floor. "May I?"

Natalia nodded. "Of course."

The dog padded over and wiped his chin before curling up on the floor at her feet and staring at the roof. "Dark in here, isn't it?" he said.

Natalia nodded again, her voice stuck behind the lump in her throat. She'd told her husband it was dark; she told everyone that it was dark in here, that the cobwebs were growing, but all they did was look at her strangely and note how spotless the ceilings were.

"Is it?" she asked the dog, quavering. "I hadn't noticed."

The dog twitched his eyebrow, managing to appear skeptical and sympathetic all at once. "I can help," he said. "If you like."

The lump in her throat melted into tears. "That… That would be nice."

He nodded, clambered to his feet, and bowed. "Good day, then," he said, and headed for the door.

Natalia's stomach leapt. "You're leaving?"

He smiled. "I'll come back."

Natalia sat cross-legged on the floor in the middle of the living room and wept. The cobwebs almost cocooned her now, hovering a scant arm's length away no matter where she went. When her husband was home it was better;

he still glowed like a flame in the dark, and the cobwebs shied away when he touched her. But he was impatient with what he called her theatrics, impatient at the growing pile of laundry and cupboards stripped bare to lay dirty offerings over stove and bench and sink.

"You could at least try something little," he'd said last night. "I'm sure it would make you feel better to accomplish something."

Probably, Natalia thought, he was right.

But moving through the cobwebs made her sick; the way they swayed and shifted in front of her, closing in behind, encircling and ensconcing and festooning her like she was a Christmas tree in need of stringing. And it had been a month since the dog had visited.

Fear hovered closer than the webs, stickier, more persistent. It stole the moisture from her mouth and slicked her hands with it instead, and whispered in her ear that things would never get better, that she would never be strong enough to burn away the webs the way her husband did, that she might as well die and save everyone the hassle.

Nodding vaguely, not quite certain what the hassle was but certain she was the cause, Natalia stood.

The webs circled and wavered before reforming closer than ever.

Natalia held a hand out in front of her and watched as tendrils of darkness darted in to lick at her fingers before melting away.

What would it be like, she wondered, to give in?

Superficially, she doubted the cobwebs would hurt her—their caresses seemed quite gentle—but instinctively she knew that they were like real webs, like spiders' webs, and that once she was in there would be no way out.

The doorbell rang, dispelling her line of thought.

Around her, the webs drew away.

Without cause, her heart began to pound. Perhaps she wanted to give in more than she liked to admit; perhaps she'd been looking forward to it, in a way, and now here was some stranger come to her door to interrupt her right at the pivotal moment.

Sighing, she went to the door and opened it. The shaggy dog sat patiently, a wooden box in his mouth.

"Oh," she greeted him again. "I'd given up on you coming back."

The dog nodded.

"Well, come in then." Natalia opened the door wide and allowed the dog in.

He trotted straight through to the living area with nary a glance at the cobwebs and sat in the middle of the room on the rug.

Natalia sat on the floor beside him. "So, what is your box?"

He placed it in her lap. "For you," he said gruffly. His gaze swept the room and he frowned. "I do hope you'll use it. This place has become positively gloomy."

And with that, he gave a flick of his tail and let himself out the front door, leaving Natalia wide-mouthed behind him, cradling the box.

She blinked. How bizarre.

She looked at the box in her hands, a rough, ugly-looking thing, all splintery and cracked.

Instinctively, she grabbed the top and tried to open it—but nothing happened. It seemed the box was just a solid cube of wood.

Anger welled in her chest and she gripped the box until her fingers hurt. What good was a horrible old box in times like these?

What was she supposed to do with

it? Burn it, so the house might see a brief, ineffectual flash of light?

The tendrils of darkness closed around Natalia's wrists and she shook. How dare the dog abuse her hope like this, especially when it was so frail as to be almost non-existent?

The tendrils tightened, and she stared at them.

Yes, they were right.

Horrible old box. Why was she even holding it?

Abruptly, she stood and stalked to the bedroom, where she bent down and shoved the box under the bed, between musty blankets and a yellowed satin dress, to languish with the dust bunnies.

Natalia lay on her bed staring at nothing.

Well, she corrected herself, the darkness wasn't precisely nothing, but it might as well be.

Her husband muttered vaguely, something perhaps about the state of the house, or his mother, or a doctor, or something…

She didn't really care.

He'd been muttering for weeks, now, and she barely noticed anymore. The cobwebs smothered the sound, just like they smothered everything else—even feeling, even fear.

That was nice, the not-feeling-fear. It was nice to be able to go an entire day without seizing up in a panic, or shying away with heart pounding and mouth dry as a tendril of darkness brushed her shoulder.

They didn't brush her anymore, the cobwebs; they surrounded her.

It was the evening after the dog had come that last time that she'd given in and let herself be cocooned, and the cobwebby tendrils had led her to her bed and laid her down, and she'd only gotten up since to visit the bathroom—and sometimes even that seemed like too much effort.

But at least the fear was gone.

That was, that is, until a dog barked.

At first Natalia ignored it, much like she ignored everything that wasn't cobwebs and tendrils and darkness these days. Darkness was, after all, all-consuming.

But the dog continued, loud enough and long enough that the darkness grew irritated.

It shuddered and snapped, cracking against Natalia's wrists, and she winced away, separating herself from the dark by a tiny fraction for the first time in weeks.

The space was just big enough for the bark to fit into, and it filtered into Natalia's ears like poison, thick and cold like dread.

Her heart squeezed in on itself and her breath caught in her throat.

Desperately, she reached out for the darkness, but still the dog barked, and the darkness writhed away.

The space grew until the bark couldn't fill it, and fear seeped in. Natalia flailed in the sheets, ankles tangled, panic rising. "No," she whimpered. "No!"

Her breath came quickly and her heart raced, and the darkness swirled around, darting and flinching, trying to regain its hold on her. Natalia lifted up her hands, trying desperately to grasp the cobwebs, but the sheets pinned her down and the bark held her back, ringing in her head like a gong.

She thrashed sideways and slipped, fell between the bed and the wall, landed on the floor with a thud.

The air rushed out of her lungs and things fell silent: the barking ceased, the darkness stilled.

Natalia gasped for breath and squeezed her eyes closed. *What am I doing?* she thought. *What is happening to me? I don't want to be afraid.*

A faint memory of something more flickered in the dark, a feeling the dog had brought.

She moved to wrap her arms around herself and as she did her elbow bumped something solid and square.

She reached out for it and winced as a splinter snagged her fingertip. The box the dog had given her. Her breath hitched again in her throat.

Grasping the box against her, Natalia struggled out from behind the bed. Her hip bashed against the bedpost and she cried out.

The cobwebs shivered.

"No!" she cried. "Don't leave me."

They circled closer.

Natalia perched on the edge of the bed, cradling the box in her lap. What was it that the dog had said? "I hope you use it." Hope, that was it: that was what the dog had brought.

But how to use it?

She turned it over in her hands, searching the surface for a clue.

She frowned. Was that a hairline crack, blending with the grain of the wood? She worried it with her nail, hissing as wood jagged in tender skin.

There, it *was* a crack, she could see it clearly now.

The darkness swirled around her, whispering and fluttering—but she didn't notice.

Natalia wedged her nail in the crack and twisted. The nail chipped, but the lid of the box popped free and Natalia shied away instinctively.

Cautiously, through slitted eyes, Natalia peered into the box.

A large steel ring, a stiff, charred piece of cloth, and a chipped bit of flint lay inside. Natalia picked up the flint and struck it against the steel without pausing to think, because that was what they were for, and so that was what you did with them.

Sparks flew. The darkness howled.

Wide-eyed, Natalia stared at it. It twisted and writhed, and the howl was both pained and angry. She lifted a hand toward it, biting her lip. She didn't want to hurt the webs.

They'd kept her safe, protected her from fear…

What was it she'd been afraid of, though, exactly?

Living, maybe—but right now she couldn't quite remember what was so horrible about life, either. Natalia looked at the flint in her hand.

Use it, the dog had said. *It's dark in here.*

Surely it wouldn't hurt to try. Natalia struck the flint, and fire flared to life.

The darkness screeched and slapped her. Natalia gasped, grabbed at the sting on her cheek as tears sprang to her eyes.

This? This was what hope did, why the dog had told her to use the box? So she could anger the darkness, provoking it to hurt her? "I'm sorry!" she cried. "I didn't mean it!"

But she had: some tiny, desperate part of her had meant to light the flame and the darkness knew.

She wailed as it lashed out again, beating her. It twined tendrils through her hair and yanked, wound its way up her nose until she couldn't breathe, crushed her body in bands of black so tight her ribs cracked.

Natalia tried to thrash, tried to escape, but the darkness held her tight and she couldn't even scream.

The flint cut into her fingers and, desperation slicing through the fear, she struck again, again, again. "Stop! Please, just stop!"

The darkness roared, thrashed at her once more—and withdrew.

When Natalia opened her eyes, the darkness hung in the corners of the ceiling like cobwebs—like it had so many months ago when the dog had first come to call.

She stared at it, breath held, waiting for it to lunge—but it stayed.

Slowly, she released her breath.

Natalia looked at the box near her feet, the steel and flint in her hands. The darkness wasn't gone—but now it would live in her house on her terms.

THE MAKING OF
THE DAY THE DOG FIRST CALLED

This story was written not long after the birth of my son. I'd only been writing seriously for a handful of years, and I didn't have enough momentum to keep it up during a bout of postnatal depression. In fact, it took writing the pitch for a non-fiction book that would eventually become the trio *How To Create Cultures, How To Create Life* and *How To Map* to really get me back into writing regularly again—but in the interim, I did manage to complete a handful of short stories, and this was one of them.

The metaphor and relevance to my then-current circumstances is, I think, obvious.

What is lovely, though, is that even in the throes of the darkness, this story still had a happy ending.

And despite discovering that the issues that I grew up dealing with were actually anxiety, which never really fully goes away, and despite at least one more serious bout of depression, I think it's safe to say the same of my life as well.

Because there is always a flint of some kind: therapy, medication, exercise, diet, all of the above or something else entirely. No matter how dark the cobwebs, somewhere, some place in your life is a flint with the power to burn them away.

You just have to take hold of the match and strike, and keep striking until the flame stays lit. <3

Read more by Amy Laurens!

A FOX OF STORMS AND STARLIGHT

CHAPTER ONE

SIX YEARS AGO, I SAVED a fox in the bush. It was only because my dog died. At the time, it felt like a pretty crappy bargain.

It was the first day of autumn—not by the calendar, but by the fresh bite in the morning air, the golden quality of the light as it lit the main road through town in the mid-afternoon.

Sailor was a big, black shaggy thing, something like a Newfoundland, a lively shadow in the golden light, and I was eleven.

I'm sorry to be starting any story this way, but the fact of the matter is, this where it all began.

I'll spare you the awful details. Enough to say that Sailor had got out of the yard somehow, and had been hit by a smallish truck careening down the highway that split our tiny town in two as it blatantly ignored the speed limit.

I saw it happen.

And although I cradled him in my lap as the smell of burnt-out brakes and hot asphalt and turning leaves filled my nose, his giant, furry black head all of him I could hold, there was nothing I could do.

There was nothing anyone could do.

I knew that, but it didn't stop the knot of frustration and guilt in my chest, or the taste of bile in the back of my throat every time I closed my eyes and saw the truck hitting him, again and again and again.

It took years for that vision to fade.

But that evening, only a few hours after it had happened, everything still felt fresh, and raw.

Sunny, my sister, was only nine at the time. She cried for hours, just sobbing like she'd never breathe right again.

I'd cried a little, at the scene with Sailor's head lying in my lap as his big, brown eye stared up at nothing.

It had been mercifully fast, there was that.

And the driver had copped a massive fine—speeding, reckless driving, I think they even defected his truck—and came to visit us later, a big, pot-bellied man standing on our front verandah, shuffling his royal blue cap round and round and round in his hands as he apologised.

But that evening, with Sunny sobbing her heart out on the couch in the living room and Mum and Dad trying desperately to console her as dinner burned on the stove, I couldn't cry, even though the acrid scent of burning soy sauce, scorching brown sugar and smoking rice wine from the marinade prickled the back of my throat and the corners of my eyes.

I was the eldest, and I had to be responsible.

Possibly, if I'd been just a little more responsible, Sailor wouldn't have died.

So I slipped out the glass slider from the family room to the deck while Sunny cried, glancing up at the two storeys of our moody grey house behind me before jumping down the three steps from the rail-less deck to the lawn, and set out for the gate in the back fence.

I couldn't cry, and I didn't want to add anything to an already chaotic and stressful situation inside—but I couldn't stay there, either.

In the gaps between the gum trees to the west, the sky tinged to red and gold at the horizon, the sun sinking slowly into oblivion. I'm pretty sure I didn't know the word oblivion back then, but I knew what it meant, how it felt—and I craved it, desperately.

Anything would be better than the gaping hole in my chest.

And so, because I didn't know where to find it or how to get there, I stalked through the bush, pushing myself until I breathed hard and my lungs ached and sweat ringed me, chasing the way that hard exercise elevated me over my constantly looping thoughts.

Directly above, dark, heavy clouds obscured the sky, and the air was thick, heavy, humid.

Beneath the smell of dry gum leaves and even drier dirt, I could catch a hint of ozone, and occasionally the wind turned cool for a breath as it gusted against my skin, promising a late evening storm.

I strode harder, faster, outpacing the video looping in my mind of the truck's impact.

When the first drops of rain spat at me from out of the sky, I barely noticed. My skin was filmed with sweat, slick and salty, and the peppering of rainwater barely added to it.

That was at first.

But within minutes, it became clear that those first pattering spits had been the early foreshadowing of a storm darker and more intense than any I remembered.

Thunder rolled across the sky, distant and grumbling at first, a lazy background chorus to the rhythmic melody of the rain as it splattered down on grey-green leaves and red-tinged twigs, turning the silvered bark of an old, dead gum to deep grey and making the spiky, tussocky grass seem oddly luminescent in the dying light.

I stood under a grey gum with stains down its trunk that the rain was turning orange, arms wrapped around myself, shivering hard—and for the briefest instant, thought about not going home.

Mum and Dad would pitch a fit.

And I had to be responsible.

I turned, dark t-shirt plastered to my skin, dark hair sticking to my face and clinging to my neck, and began trudging my way back.

The storm closed over properly, clouds rolling over the horizon and cutting off the thin scythe of blood-coloured sunset, making the bush dark and unwelcoming in the premature night.

Lightning flashed.

Thunder cracked hot on its heels.

I jumped—and stared hard at the gap between two ghost-barked trees, where for a second, I was sure I'd seen a pair of eyes.

Nothing moved.

Nothing except the drenching rain, anyway, weighing down the branches that tossed fitfully in the wind.

My pulse slowly calmed.

The rumours we'd all grown up with, indoctrinated since both, spoke of something strange and dark… but in the forest north of here, in the pines, the plantation—not here, not in the natural, native bush.

I shivered.

The smell of wet dirt and soaked bark rose around me, undercut by eucalypt and ozone.

If anything had the power to wash away the hurt inside me, this storm was it. I tipped my face to the sky, imagining that the rain washing over me had the ability to wash me inside as well, and the raindrops splattered hard on my cheekbones, my chin, my tightly closed eyelids.

More lightning. More thunder, cracking over the constant hiss of the falling rain.

And in the distance, something eerie, lifting the hairs on the back of my neck: a strange kind of high-pitched howl, a cry that rang with moonlight and distance, cutting straight through the noise of the storm.

Bolts of lightning streaked across the sky—one—two—three—in the space of half a second, followed immediately by a growling crack of thunder so immense it vibrated in my chest.

I ducked down instinctively into a crouch.

There, in the corner of my eye…

I froze, crouched with my arms over my head.

The strange cries came again—and they were closer.

I stared hard at the place, low to the ground, where I was sure I'd seen something small, maybe the size of a cat.

Flash. Growl.

Rain spitting down.

There. Right there. A small animal, pointy ears, light coloured chin and throat…

The strange, eerie cries came a third time, and my heart pounded fiercely. Whatever was making the noise, it was close. Really close.

The little creature across from me reacted too, flattening itself to the ground.

My jaw twitched.

My heart pounded.

My fingertips bit into my upper arms.

Stay? Go?

Run? Freeze?

The hairs on my neck prickled again and goosebumps broke out all over me.

Cold dread formed a knot in my stomach.

Something was coming.

Something worse than the storm.

I had to get home.

I made it halfway to standing—and a series of strange, awful noises made me freeze again. They were sharp, clacking, squealing sounds, like someone knocking two echoing stones against each other, interspersed with high-pitched yowling...

The creature in the darkness screamed.

I threw my back against the gumtree behind me, pressing hard against it.

My heart hammered.

I peered back and forth in the dark, eyes wide.

Rain drenched down, but my throat was dry.

My pulse pounded faster.

The little creature screamed again—and as lightning flashed, I saw it on its back, legs slashing wildly as something attacked.

The awful, clicking-yowling noises sounded right in front of me.

I slapped my hands over my ears, gasping. Water ran down my face, getting into my mouth, my eyes.

It was hurting.

Whatever the small thing was, it was getting hurt, and I'd seen enough animals hurting today.

Something in my chest snapped.

I flung myself across the ground, leaping a couple of tussocks and a fallen branch before I crashed to my knees.

I crawled closer, desperate, gasping for air through the heavy curtains of rain.

I couldn't see it. Where?

Somewhere here, near the base of that tree...

The yowling screeched right next to my ear. I cowered against the ground, spiky grass pricking my face, wet-earth smell smothering me—but now, there was a strange mustiness too, a cousin to wet-dog smell.

At the next flash of lightning, I saw it.

The creature was a fox—and something barely visible was attacking it, only the gleam of eye or flicker of teeth visible in the gloom.

But the damage was real enough.

The little fox's side had been opened right up, and in the bright, stark flashes of heavenly electricity, the blood was dark, thinned by the constant rain.

No. No more animals were going to die today.

Not when this time, I could do something about it.

I snatched at a branch on the ground that turned out to be more of a glorified twig, and launched myself toward the creature.

I had no idea what was attacking it, but I screamed and waved my handful of twiggy leaves anyway, batting them in the air over the fox like I knew what I was doing.

The horrible clacking cries ceased abruptly.

With one long, low rumble, the rain began to ebb.

I poised, waiting.

But nothing came.

The attackers were gone.

Still gasping for air, pulse galloping in my throat, I sat next to the fox and shifted it carefully into my lap, realising as I tasted salt that I was crying.

I huddled over, trying to shelter the poor creature from the slackening rain, running my fingers over its wiry cheek— over and over and over and over.

"Please," I sobbed, throat tight and aching, chest constricted. "Please. Please don't die. Please."

Please, I prayed to anything that might be listening. *No more death. Not today.*

Not today.

Another gust of cool air washed over the clearing, taking the last of the rain with it—and lifting the goose-bumps on my arms again.

And as it did, I could have sworn I heard a voice. *Neither do I wish him to die now.*

I shivered, drawing the fox close, like it was a stuffed animal I could hug for comfort—its comfort or mine, I couldn't say. I glanced around the dripping bush, eyes wide. The rumours spoke of an evil presence, and I could easily believe that might be what had attacked the fox.

But a voice? No one had ever mentioned a voice.

There was nothing to be seen, and anyway the voice had sounded kindly— and didn't want the fox to die.

Assuming I hadn't just imagined it, of course. Which, half-drowned by grief, the other half drowned by the storm... An over-active imagination seemed highly likely.

Can you fix him? I thought it hard, though, just in case someone really was listening.

Something shifted in my lap.

Around us, the world stilled, dazed from the storm, but also something more, something watching, something waiting, as the bush held its collective breath.

The only sound was the occasional drip of rainwater from the gum leaves onto a fallen log—no insects, no wind, no rustling of leaves.

Just… stillness.

And the fox, who shivered in my lap.

The clouds tore open, revealing a ragged triangle of stars that glittered in the fox's eye as it blinked open and stared up at me.

My chest snagged.

My throat ached from crying, and a headache was forming in the back of my head.

But the fox blinked up at me—alive.

I ran a finger down it again, from nose to cheek to ear to shoulder, all the way down its side to its thick, bushy tail—and the wound in its side began to close.

Laboriously, it hauled itself to its front legs.

I tried to stop it—"No, it's okay, you can stay here, I'll look after you"—but it lifted its top lip to show half-hearted teeth, and staggered away.

As it did, I thought perhaps its fur began to shrink.

And suddenly, it looked larger in the night—as large as a dog, as large as Sailor…

But I blinked, and it was just a trick of the light, because the creature that darted away into the bushes like nothing was wrong at all was clearly a fox, the size of a large cat or maybe a small beagle, and nothing more.

And if something screamed in the night not long afterward, and the cry sounded horribly, horribly human?

Well.

I was halfway back toward home again by then, and I pressed my fingertips to my lower eyelids and prayed my parents wouldn't murder me for getting home so late.

Keep reading! Head to
www.inkprintpress.com/amylaurens/
stormfoxes/fox/
to buy your copy now!

ABOUT THE AUTHOR

AMY LAURENS is an Australian author of fantasy fiction for all ages. She hopes very much that you have some identifiable flints in your life; if you are having trouble spotting them, you might consider calling your local mental health hotline? <3

Amy has also written the award-winning portal-fantasy *Sanctuary* series about Edge, a 13-year-old girl forced to move to a small country town because of witness protection (the first book is *Where Shadows Rise*), the humorous fantasy *Kaditeos* series, following newly graduated Evil Overlord Mercury as she attempts to acquire a castle, the young adult series *Storm Foxes*, about love and magic and family in small town Australia, and a whole host of non-fiction.

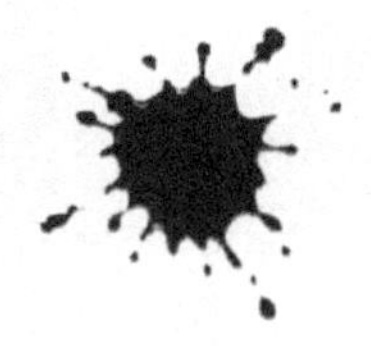

INKLETS

Collect them all! Released on the 1st and 15th of each month.

INKLET #055
Allure
AMY LAURENS

The LIES We KNOW
LIANA BROOKS

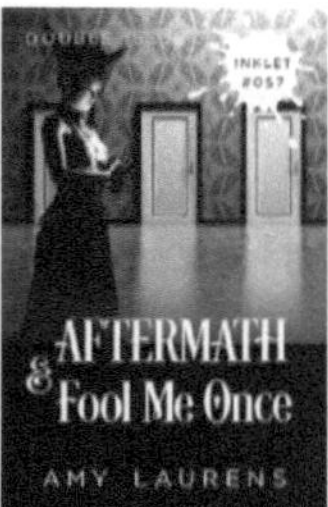

AFTERMATH & Fool Me Once
AMY LAURENS

Purity
An Age Of Unicorns Story
AMY LAURENS

Saved
AMY LAURENS

A Kiss is the Secret
AMY LAURENS

A Changing Tides Story
Fire Bright
AMY LAURENS

Hades AND Persephone
LIANA BROOKS

Just So Long As You're Happy
AMY LAURENS

INKLET #064
Theft Of A Lifetime
LIANA BROOKS

INKLET #065
Shoe
AMY LAURENS

INKLET #066
Published AUTHOR
LIANA BROOKS

DOUBLE ISSUE
INKLET #067
THE REMARKABLE INSIGHT OF JELLYBEANS, & Understanding
AMY LAURENS

INKLET #068
Desperate Measures
AMY LAURENS

INKLET #069
Rock-a-bye
LIANA BROOKS

INKLET #070
the Other Carly
AMY LAURENS

INKLET #071
Bs By Bioluminescent Light
AMY LAURENS

INKLET #072
Even Villains Grant Wishes
A Heroes & Villains Story
LIANA BROOKS